AuthorHouse™
1663 Liberty Drive
Bloomington, IN 47403
www.authorhouse.com
Phone: 833-262-8899

Because of the dynamic nature of the Internet, any web addresses or links contained in this book may have changed since publication and may no longer be valid. The views expressed in this work are solely those of the author and do not necessarily reflect the views of the publisher, and the publisher hereby disclaims any responsibility for them.

This book is printed on acid-free paper.

ISBN: 978-1-6655-4928-8 (sc)
ISBN: 978-1-6655-4929-5 (e)

Library of Congress Control Number: 2022900506

Print information available on the last page.

Published by AuthorHouse 01/24/2022

authorHOUSE®

written and illustrated by
Ashlin Aimee

for Dora, Theo and Charlie
because I miss you while you are at school
-Mom

hi, I'm Quinn!

Tomorrow is my first day of school. I'm really excited, but I'm a little bit nervous too...

Oh, I mean, I'm 5 years old. I'm not scared of anything!

Well, maybe I am just a teensy bit worried... but, uh-about my mom. I wonder what she is going to do without me all day.

1

I wonder if my mom will be lonely driving by herself...

I wonder if my mom will have a hard time listening to her teacher...

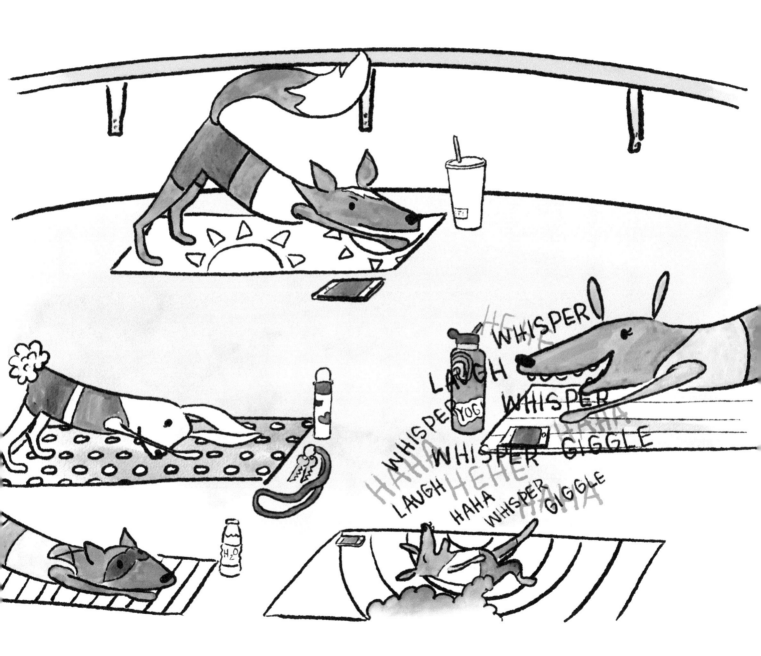

I wonder if my mom will remember to clean up her own messes...

I wonder if my mom will eat all of her veggies at lunch...

I wonder if my mom will have a lot of work to get done...

I wonder if my mom will be able to take a break and rest...

13

I wonder if my mom will be brave when she tries something new...

I wonder if my mom will make something to show me when I get home...

16

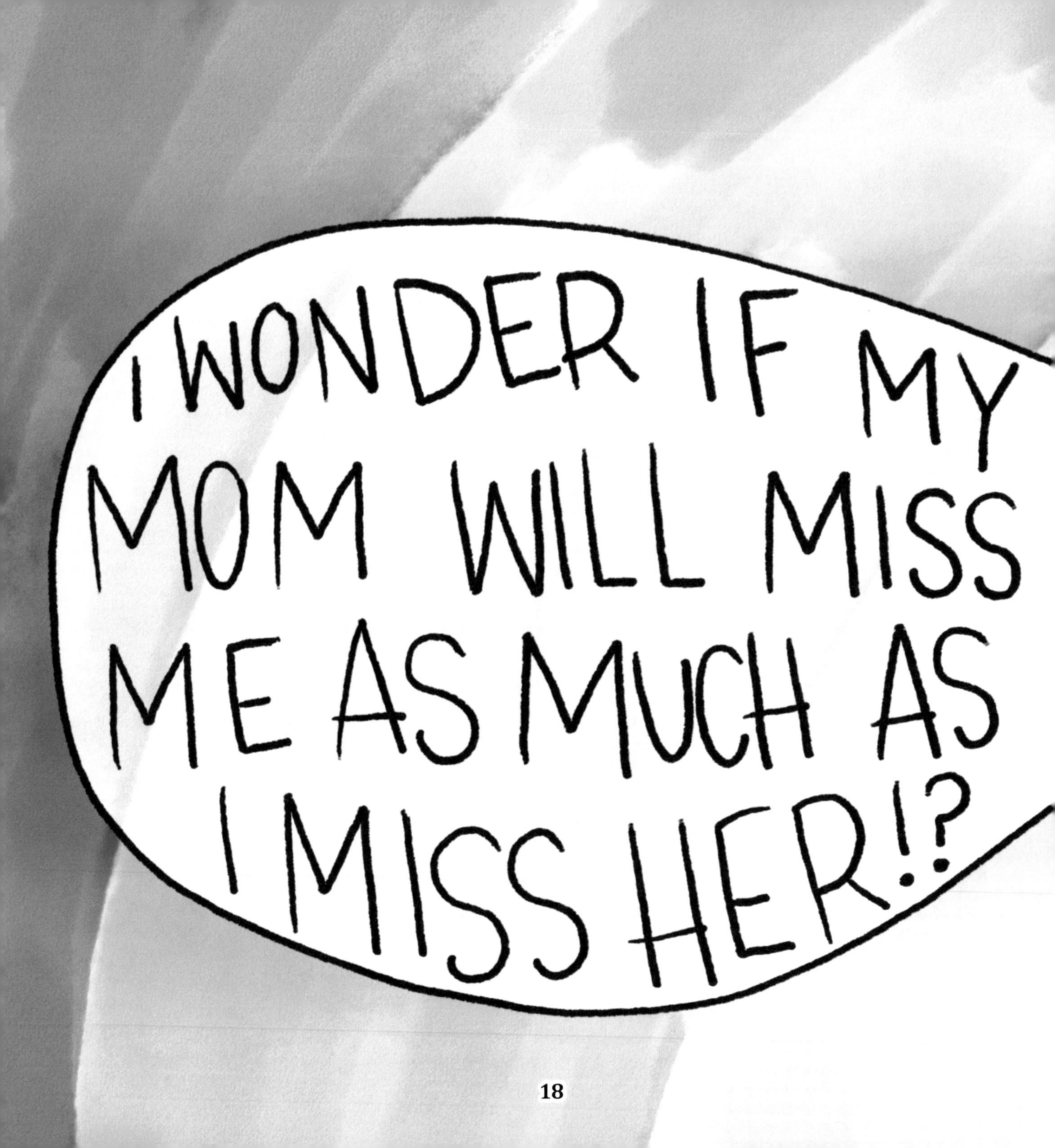
I WONDER IF MY MOM WILL MISS ME AS MUCH AS I MISS HER!?

20

I had a great 1st day!

and I think my mom did too!

Maybe I didn't need to worry about going to school after all.

I'm going- I mean, my mom is going to be just fine.

24

Printed in the United States
by Baker & Taylor Publisher Services